MW01146389

THE GIANT BABY

Laurie Foos is the author of the novels *Ex Utero*, *Portrait of the Walrus by a Young Artist*, *Twinship*, *Bingo Under the Crucifix*, and *Before Elvis There Was Nothing*. "Moon Pies," from her sixth novel, *The Blue Girl*, received the second place 2008 Italo Calvino Fiction Award.

First published by GemmaMedia in 2012.

GemmaMedia
230 Commercial Street
Boston, MA 02109 USA

www.gemmamedia.com

© 2012 by Laurie Foos

Printed in the United States of America

978-1-936846-29-0

Library of Congress Cataloging-in-Publication Data

Foos, Laurie
    The giant baby / Laurie Foos.
        p. cm. — (Gemma open door)
    ISBN 978-1-936846-29-0
    1. Married people—Fiction. 2. Gardens—Fiction.
3. Fantasy fiction. I. Title.
    PS3556.O564G53 2012
    813'.54—dc23
2012031758

Cover by Night & Day Design

Inspired by the Irish series of books designed for adult literacy, Gemma Open Door Foundation provides fresh stories, new ideas, and essential resources for young people and adults as they embrace the power of reading and the written word.

Brian Bouldrey
North American Series Editor

GEMMA

Open Door

ONE

We should have known when we grew the baby that things would turn out the way they did. Earl and I, we never should have thought we could get away with having any kind of baby, never mind a giant baby like the one we grew out in the garden. We never had any luck. Not in that garden of ours, at least. We planted tomatoes, and they turned into pomegranates. We planted corn, but the ears split and bloomed into cabbage leaves. And the carrots, oh, the carrots. Down in the ground we dug, and up came some of the longest and thickest cucumbers we'd ever seen.

Sometimes I forget that things aren't the same for other people as they are for

Earl and me. Sometimes I even forget that there are other people out there, that they exist. People who plant one thing and grow another. People who have no interest in seeds or don't even have a garden. I forget that there is anyone but Earl and me now that the giant baby is gone. He was the one thing we grew that we had hope for.

It wasn't that we didn't love the giant baby or think of him as ours, as belonging to us. He didn't grow inside me, the way most babies grow inside their mothers, but this is a new world we live in. Some babies grow in dishes in labs, and some in the bellies of other women who then give the baby they've grown to its mother. There are all kinds of ways that babies grow, and so what if the way we grew ours wasn't what you'd call "conventional"?

So what?

So what, we said, Earl and I. Who would possibly care that our baby was not grown inside a woman, but in the garden where we planted him?

He grew in our yard near the raspberries that turned into radishes and the orange tree that collapsed under the weight of the pumpkins that sprouted among the leaves. Who would possibly care what we did in the privacy of our own yard? Who was anyone to say that what we did was wrong?

We grew the baby in the yard. We grew him, Earl and I, and we loved him—I think we really did—like he was ours because he *was* ours.

Until he wasn't anymore.

TWO

It all started with the toes.

But I should explain. I have some explaining to do, just like Ricky used to say to Lucy on the old *I Love Lucy* show when Lucy got busted (always) for trying to find herself a part in one of Ricky's cabaret shows where he sang the "Babalu." That Lucy, always getting caught with fruit piled on her head or grapes between her toes, trying to wind her way onstage with Ricky. And he caught her every time, and would say in that accent of his that she had some "'splaining to do." But I didn't understand what there was to explain. Why didn't Ricky get it? All Lucy ever wanted was more time with Ricky.

Earl and I were like Lucy and Ricky in that way, I guess. We were always trying to be together more, or more together somehow. I'd fallen in love with Earl the minute I'd heard his name.

"The name's Earl," he said to me that day at the vegetable stand, when he reached for a carton of cherry tomatoes at the same second I did. I looked down at his hand on top of mine, our two hands both covering the redness of the cherry tomatoes, and I blushed in a way I hadn't blushed for years.

"Earl," I said. "Earl."

I repeated the name to him as if I weren't sure I'd heard him right. I remember letting the name rest in my mouth as if I were tasting it. You don't meet many men named Earl anymore.

I'd always wanted to meet a man named Earl, though I hadn't known it until the second he'd introduced himself. *Earl*, I thought, *such a solid name*. The kind of name you could count on. What had happened to all the solid names of the past? Short bursts of men's names like Chuck or Ed or Burt. Or Earl.

I said to myself as I took the little basket of cherry tomatoes he handed to me, *I'm going to fall in love with a man named Earl and grow a whole life with him someday.*

And that's just how it happened. We left that vegetable stand and have been together ever since. Even when Earl had to be away from me to work at the lumber yard, I could still feel him inside of me. I thought of that feeling as the

"Essence of Earl," and it was that feeling that we brought to the house we built and to the garden we grew together. Sometimes I thought that if I could open Earl up and climb my way inside of him and stay in there, in the innards of Earl, I would. At night when we slept, I'd curl up next to Earl and press my face into his back and whisper to myself, *Oh, sweet Essence of Earl, let me get inside.*

And Earl would press his back harder against me, as if he could feel it, too, and wanted me in there, the two of us folded over each other, skin over skin and bone to bone, muscle and heart and blood that pumped.

But that was before everything happened, when we were just Earl and Linda and no one else.

Earl had gone to the garden that day without me, the way he sometimes would after he was fired from the lumberyard. Poor Earl had sold the wrong kind of wood to a couple who built a deck that collapsed after a party. A highly intoxicated and obese man had done a cannonball into the pool that the deck surrounded. There had been a lawsuit. The man—whom the lawyers always called obese instead of huge or fat and intoxicated instead of drunk—had splinters in places that splinters are never meant to prick through, Earl reported to me on the day he was let go.

"The boss just looked at me and said, 'Damn it, Earl, if you don't know the difference between cedar and untreated pine by now, may God save your sorry soul,'" Earl said as we stood at the window that overlooked the backyard. We stared out at the broken pumpkin tree.

I told him that, to my mind, no obese drunken man should attempt a cannonball without thinking of the consequences beforehand.

"Splinters or no splinters, that's just downright irresponsible," I said, and Earl pulled me closer and pressed his nose into my hair.

"Oh, Linda," he said, "if only the whole world could see things the way you do. But I've got no business selling wood anyway, when all I want is to be out with you in the garden."

We had pumpkin soup in bread bowls that night for dinner, and a few weeks later Earl found the toes while I lay on the Barcalounger reading the seed catalogue. We hadn't planted anything new in a while, and, for a time, we'd cut our losses. We'd taken the soil to the nearby garden center and had the soil tested. "Ph perfect," they pronounced it, with nothing showing too much acid or fungus or whatever it is they look for when they test people's soil. Sometimes I wonder what makes a person decide to go into the business of soil testing, but then I think: who am I to judge? I grew a baby in my backyard.

I have no room to talk.

I had my tea on the end table next to me and my knees curled up under the coverlet. I was reading about flowers, thinking that maybe if Earl and I planted flowers rather than fruits or vegetables we would have a change of luck. I imagined roses the size of lanterns, Earl and I trimming and weeding and tending the way we'd imagined we would when we'd started the garden years ago. I closed my eyes and imagined Earl and me standing barefoot in the soil, the smell of roses so strong we had to cover our mouths to drown it out. I could almost feel the dirt under my feet as I lay back in the lounger. The seed catalog fell to the floor as I closed my eyes and thought of roses that would wind their way around my arms and my legs, up through my hair, the vines and thorns twisting my hair into braids.

When I opened my eyes, there was Earl with this look on his face. It was a look I'd never seen before, not even after the accident with the backhoe that had sealed our childlessness forever.

"For God's sake, Earl," I said, "you didn't hurt yourself, did you?"

I was worried about Earl. He hadn't been the same since the firing, or, before that, since the backhoe ruined him in ways a man shouldn't be ruined. It wasn't something we talked about, the day he'd gotten himself run over by the backhoe, but the memory of it lingered. It did. We hadn't wanted babies all that much, and I was older now, too old. One day a woman from town stopped me at the grocery store and told me that she hadn't seen me looking this thin before, and was I dieting or working out.

"Working out?" I asked, and she said, "Yes, Linda, you know, with weights and all." When I said that I hadn't been, unless you counted being out in the garden on my hands and knees, she said no, gardening never made anyone look so lean.

"Oh, that's it then," she'd said, "you're just getting old."

I was thinking about that neighbor woman and the day Earl had been bloodied by the backhoe, the stitches and the ice packs, when Earl sat down on the edge of the Barcalounger and told me to close my eyes.

"Promise me, Linda," he said, his voice low as he leaned closer to me, his hands clasped one on top of the other. "Promise me you won't open them until I say."

I pressed my hands into my thin arms and felt the muscles and bones sticking out of me, the veins, too, and thought that the neighbor woman was right. I was getting old.

"Earl, what is it?" I said. "You're scaring me now."

He kept his hands squeezed tightly together and smiled with one side of his mouth slightly higher than the other, his best Earl smile, the one he gave only to me. To hell with that woman, I thought. I might have been getting old, but I still had this.

"Close your eyes now, just like I said," he told me, and as I closed my eyes I could hear the breath in his chest moving in and out, little hisses that had helped me sleep for all these years.

"Don't look," he said. "Don't look until I say."

I closed my eyes and kept them closed. I kept my promise to Earl and did not open them again until he told me to. I don't know what I was expecting to see but when I opened my eyes, I knew that I hadn't been prepared for what I was about to see.

He told me to open my eyes, and when I did, he parted his hands and sat there cradling the things he had brought in from the garden.

Toes. Baby's toes. Ten of them, and not just bones, but pink skin and impossibly tiny nails.

I looked up at Earl, and he looked back at me. I cupped my hands as he poured the toes into my palms.

"Are these what I think they are?" I

whispered, and Earl nodded, folding one hand over the two of mine.

"From the garden," he said.

I stared down at those perfectly formed miniature toes and felt them grow warm in my hands. Slowly I counted them over and over, one through ten, marveling at the shape of each toe, the plumpness of the big toes, the splendor of the pinkies.

"Our luck is about to change," he said, and I didn't answer him. I kept holding the toes and wondering what was going to happen to us now that the garden that we thought had turned against us had now risen up and sent us ten baby's toes.

THREE

Of course we planted them.

Of course we did. What else would we do?

It was like that old saying, that when the world sends you lemons, you make lemonade. The world sent us baby's toes, and we saw nothing to do but plant them.

We never thought of any other possibilities. I guess other people might have. Other people might have imagined horrible things about a baby cut up, dismembered, and thrown in our garden, but Earl and I had never been much like other people.

Lucy and Ricky would have planted them, too. I feel sure of that, even now when I watch reruns. If Lucy found toes in the earth in her garden, she would have called for Ricky. He might have said she had some 'splainin' to do, but they would have planted them all the same.

The world sent us baby's toes, and we never thought of sadness. The world sent us baby's toes, and we rejoiced.

The next morning we woke up at dawn and got ready to plant. Neither of us had our morning coffee or even brushed our teeth. I picked up the shoe box on the bureau next to the bed where I'd placed the toes the night before. I'd wrapped them in a pair of Earl's socks to keep them safe. It had been hard to sleep with the toes there beside me, but I'd kept my eyes closed and held on to Earl all through the night, pressing myself against his back.

We walked across the lawn in our bare feet. It seemed like the right thing to do. If we were going to plant toes, there was no sense in wearing shoes. I felt the wetness of the grass under my feet as we made our way across the lawn. Earl held his arm around my shoulders, and I kept the shoe box close to my chest.

You might say I cradled it.

Earl opened the gate that he'd built out of excess wood from the lumberyard. I thought of the day he'd brought the wood home, the excitement we felt as he unloaded it from the pickup truck his boss had lent him. I thought of that lopsided smile of his as he'd gone about the business of hammering the wood into place, how he'd laughed when the gate swung back and forth just the way it was supposed to. I thought, too, of the day the backhoe had gone berserk, the blood running down the front of his cargo shorts. But then I stopped myself from thinking those thoughts and clutched the shoe box.

We got down on our knees together in the dirt and Earl dug with the spade. Neither of us was sure how deep the hole should be, but when Earl could lean down on his fists so the dirt was level with his elbows, we agreed that was deep enough.

"Is there something we should say?" I whispered. Earl took the shoe box from me and unwrapped the toes from his pair of argyle socks. "I feel like we should say something."

He held the toes in his hands and bowed his head.

"Maybe you should be the one," he said.

"But you found them."

In the end we did it together. I took five of the toes, Earl took the other five, and together we scooped them into the earth. Together we told the garden that we loved it in spite of itself, that we welcomed the cabbage the size of soccer balls and the zucchini that wound itself into vines of sour grapes.

"And we promise," I whispered to the garden as Earl covered the last of the toes with soil, "to love whatever it is you decide to send us."

Earl lay the spade down in the dirt and kissed me, hard, on the mouth.

"Amen," he said.

I took Earl's hand and felt the dirt on

his palm moving against the dirt in mine as if it were doing some sort of dance. I squeezed so hard that he winced as he closed the gate behind us. I kept squeezing his hand even after we crawled back into bed and lay together with the soil still on our feet. The dirt made scratching sounds as Earl and I rubbed our feet together under the bedding. We fell into a fitful sleep that lasted three days. We held on to each other, pulling, squeezing each other even in sleep, as if we couldn't get close enough no matter how tightly we held on.

While we slept I dreamed of babies. A sea of babies beneath us, holding us up, and Earl and I floating on the mattress above them. Hundreds of babies lifting us over their baby heads, Earl and

I swimming on the mattress, kicking our feet in rhythm as we sailed in the bed with the babies below us.

"Holy crap, Earl," I said in the dream, "would you look at all these babies?"

But Earl said nothing. I woke up several times in a sweat only to have Earl pull me closer, ever closer, as if he were the one trying to get inside me and not the other way around, the way it had always been. Every time I closed my eyes the baby dreams started up again until I woke up on the third day, finally, to the sounds of crying.

FOUR

Looking back now, I wonder what we expected to find that day. We knew so little about babies, even when we were much younger and the possibility of having babies still sometimes lurked. It wasn't that we didn't want children, but rather that we just never seemed to get around to having them. We'd always liked things the way they'd been. Earl and me, me and Earl. Just us.

"Just us," we'd say to the waitress at the diner in town when we'd head in on Sunday mornings for the special.

The waitress would smile and lead us to a booth in the back, a quiet spot far from the family tables up front filled with kids spitting straws at each other and babies banging spoons on the tables. The sound would ring out through the diner, but in the back room with Earl, we'd reach for each other's hands across the table and sigh at the quiet.

"You two aren't like other couples," the waitress told us one Sunday when she'd brought us some cheese danishes to go in a box. "On the house," she said. "You seem to really like each other."

We laughed, but it was true, we realized, as we walked out of the diner, looking at the other couples with the straw-spitting kids and banging spoons. We didn't scowl at each other or sit in ugly silence. We didn't have worry lines on our foreheads and between our eyebrows. We just did our best being us, because it seemed the one thing we knew how to do. We thought this every night as we climbed into bed and went about the business of trying to climb inside each other.

Until children became impossible. And of course, somewhere along the way, I'd gotten old.

That morning when the crying started we had to peel ourselves apart. My hands had glued themselves to Earl's back and made a sucking sound when I pried them off. Earl's head had somehow found its way into the crook of my shoulder, and when he pulled his head back, he screamed as a chunk of hair remained stuck on the upper part of my left arm.

I fell off the bed and stumbled to the dresser to grab a sweater and a pair of jeans. The crying grew louder as we hurried into our clothes, Earl tripping over his sweatpants and landing flat on the carpet outside the bedroom.

"Earl, honey, take it easy now," I said, scrambling to help him to his feet. "Whatever's out there is going to wait for us."

Pins and needles raced through my feet as I tottered behind him. Earl grabbed my arm and pulled me toward the back door.

"Do you hear that?" he said, almost in a scream. "That's a baby's cry. That is a baby crying for us, right now, right out there."

He stopped and held his hand on

the doorknob. We looked at each other and nodded. I felt my breath dry in my throat, felt a rawness there that ached every time another cry rang out.

A cry for us, I thought, the two of us running now, barefoot in the backyard toward the gate in the distance. *A cry for Earl and me.*

The gate slapped back as Earl ran ahead, his feet tromping over the would-be-tomatoes turned to radish and the lettuce heads turned to watermelon vines. For a moment, in the space between cries, I felt a surge of panic in my chest. What if I didn't know what to do, how to take care of it? What if that was the reason we'd never had children? What if we were unfit?

I thought of all these things as I

stumbled after Earl, over the watermelon vines and toward the pumpkin tree. I stopped when I saw Earl drop to his knees in front of me.

"Oh, Linda," he said, so softly I could hardly hear it, "oh, come and look."

I closed my eyes. I'll admit that much now. When Earl first accused me of not wanting to look at the baby that morning, I told him he had no right to judge me, and besides, his back had been turned. But now, after all that's happened, I can admit that I wasn't sure I was ready to see.

When I opened them, I dropped next to Earl on the dirt. In the hole Earl had dug a few nights before lay the tiniest baby I'd ever seen. Of course, I hadn't seen or held many babies before our own grew, but I knew this one was on the smaller side. Tiny, but perfect, with round cheeks the color of the sunset and a crown of reddish hair that circled high above the palest of brows. I felt a pulling sensation in my middle as I looked at him—he was fully formed, tiny as he was—that made me want to shout out to the world that I was not old.

"Where are his feet?" I said to Earl, crawling around to the other side of the hole to get a better look. "I can't see his feet."

Earl reached down into the hole and cupped the tiny feet in his hands. The baby had stopped crying now and breathed in shallow bursts that made a sighing sound through his parted lips.

"He's all here, don't you worry," Earl

said, and together we counted his ten fingers and toes, laughing together as the baby sighed.

We sat cross-legged and stared down into the hole in the ground that the baby did not quite fill. Finally, when I'd had enough of looking and the stabbing in my stomach flared up again, I reached down into the hole.

"What are you doing?" Earl said.

I laughed and clucked my tongue. I actually clucked it. So many times I'd heard mothers make this gentle sound. It was as if to say, *What are you worried about? I've got this. Now and forever, I've got this.* Until I made that clucking sound myself, I hadn't known that I'd been waiting to make it.

"Oh, Earl," I said, "You act like you've never seen a baby before."

We both laughed a little, quietly, but then as I reached one hand behind the baby's head and the other under his back and moved to pull him up, we stopped.

"What's wrong?" he said.

I tried again to lift the baby, and again the baby would not come.

"I don't know," I said, and moved to the other side of the hole. "Bad leverage, maybe."

I switched hands, the left hand now under the head and the right supporting the body, and moved to lift again.

But nothing.

"He's stuck."

"No, he's not stuck, just pull harder."

"You try it, then."

"All right, move over, I'll get him out."

"Be careful of his head, Earl, be sure to hold the head."

"Jeez, Linda, I think I can figure out that much."

"Here, let me help. On three. One, two…"

"You're right. He's stuck."

"I told you he was stuck."

FIVE

Except he wasn't stuck, or at least not wedged in, as most people would think the word *stuck* implies. Part of him was still attached to the ground, and only after we kept pushing and pulling and finally digging with our hands did we see the thin white vines that held him to the ground.

"Roots," Earl said. "He's rooted."

I didn't answer. I just sat in the dirt and held my stomach, which was now beginning to burn, a slow, almost delicious burning that rose up from my belly and into my chest.

"Maybe we should pull harder," Earl said, as I felt the tingling in my chest flare up and then disappear.

"No, I don't think so," I said.

I looked over at the half-collapsed pumpkin tree that was supposed to deliver us oranges. I thought about the first time we'd tried to grow anything in our garden, how we'd driven down to the garden center and bought some packets of herbs. Fresh basil leaves, *guaranteed to grow*, the packet read. I'd imagined myself cooking pasta for Earl on Saturday nights with basil fresh from our garden and cherry tomatoes as garnishes, a symbol of the way we'd come together that day at the vegetable stand. How happy Earl would look, how satisfied. Only our seeds had burrowed themselves into the ground and come up as thick bunches of celery with roots so deep they trailed halfway across the yard.

"That's it," I said, and reminded Earl of the celery roots that had torn through half of the lawn. "He's not done growing yet. He needs some more time."

"And what do we do in the meantime? Do we just leave him out here to grow?"

"I don't know what we do, Earl," I said. "I really don't."

SIX

We left him to grow. There was no other choice.

At first we checked on him every couple of minutes, but after the initial crying, the baby fell asleep and stayed that way all day. Once or twice I tried again to lift him because it was the only thing to ease that burning in my stomach. But he wouldn't come. By evening our backs were wrenched from crouching down in the dirt to watch him.

"Should we go inside?" Earl asked.

I sat half-crouched, half-lying on the ground and looked over at Earl, who was covered in dirt. Smears lined his brow, muddy prints covered his arms and hands.

"I guess," I said. "I guess we ought to."

As we got up and crept carefully past the sleeping, rooted baby, I thought about all those families at the diner that we saw every Sunday. Why hadn't I ever stopped to look at them, really look? Why had Earl and I always been in such a hurry to hide ourselves off in the corner to be alone? We were alone all the time. I saw that now. Why hadn't we taken the time to sit next to a family filled with children and just watch them, take in everything they ate and did?

I didn't know the answer. I'm not sure I know even now. Lucy and Ricky had gone on to have a baby, after all. Lucy had to change her ways and get the neighbor woman to babysit Little Ricky all the time. But the show had never been the same as it had been with just Lucy and Ricky, I realized, as Earl and I crossed the lawn and went back into the house. The show had never been as good once the baby came along.

Inside we ate and ate and ate some more. I threw open the cupboards and cooked with what can only be called abandon. I baked pumpkin pies and made sauce from the giant tomatoes. I made salads filled with cabbage leaves that had ballooned into globes and chopped up enormous celery stalks. Ever since the garden had started to grow things, Earl and I had been cautious in our eating. But now all that was over, and we ate at the dining room table with our hands, shoveling in the rhubarb and deformed eggplant, eating as much of what we'd grown as our stomachs would allow.

When the eating was over, we sat and looked at each other over the sea of plates that covered the table.

"That's it!" I said suddenly.

My outburst startled Earl, and he jumped up, banging the area that the backhoe had attacked. He whimpered and held his hands there. Normally I would have rushed over to massage the area or even run to the refrigerator for a pack of ice, but now I had other things to think about. Things other than Earl.

"He needs to eat," I said, "or how else can he grow?"

I ran into the kitchen for the biggest basket I could find. Together we filled the basket to the brim with the vegetable

and fruits we still had left in the cupboards: turnips meant to be thyme, blue-
berries that we'd planted as rosemary,
potatoes whose seed packets had prom-
ised the sweetest sage.

Earl heaved the basket up on one
shoulder as I held the back door open
for him. I stood there for just a moment
and watched him walking ahead of me,
the basket filled with food for the baby—
our baby—balanced on his arm, his right
hand gripping the top. I stood there in
the doorway for just a minute or so and
thought, *There goes Earl, my strong, solid
Earl,* the man I made up my mind to fall
in love with as soon as I'd heard his name.
I let myself have that moment, watching
him there in the doorway. Then I hurried

behind him to catch up, stopping only when the basket fell off Earl's shoulder as if in slow motion, cabbage and corn and butternut squash tumbling out and rolling into the pumpkin tree, the whole garden littered with vegetables.

"What in the world...?" I heard Earl say just before he dropped to his knees.

There was the baby, right where we'd left him, only he wasn't tiny anymore. The hole in the ground had sealed itself shut. In the time it had taken us to eat, the baby had grown. When Earl stood up again I estimated the infant to be about waist-high. He looked at me and smiled, and I saw his full body—I could see for sure he was a boy—with roots shooting out of his back and into the place where we'd planted him. I tried to smile back at it—at him—but just as I did, the baby opened up its mouth and started to scream.

SEVEN

I'm not exactly sure what happened next, because by the account that Earl gave to me later, I passed out right there in the garden.

When I came to I saw Earl's face, still covered in dirt, hovering over mine. He held a jar of menthol cream he'd sometimes used when he caught a nasty cold in the days before he'd been fired at the lumberyard, when Earl spent his time outside and not here in the house with me. For a minute when I woke up, I thought we were back in those days again, and I wanted nothing more than to press myself against Earl's chest and breathe it in, that Essence of Earl, that smell that sustained me through all those years of just being us.

But then I heard the sound of screaming and the pelting of the rain on the roof, and I remembered.

"He grew," I said, which I knew was obvious, but I couldn't think of anything else to say. What else could anyone say when a waist-high baby now stood in her garden?

"Yes, he did," Earl said. He wiped his face with the back of his sleeve, smearing more dirt over his mouth and nose. "A whole lot."

I sat up from the pillow and listened to the pounding of the rain. Earl pulled the covers down and got in beside me but didn't reach for me the way he usually did. The dirt was everywhere by then, on the bed sheets, the pillowcase, even on the night stand. I couldn't think of a time we'd gotten into that bed together when Earl hadn't reached for me, even after the backhoe incident. For the first time since I'd met Earl—my solid, dependable, grow-a-life-with-me Earl—I felt afraid.

Of course, the screaming didn't help. The screams the baby let out did not sound at all like those of a newborn, those short, punctuated bursts of wanting that even women who aren't mothers can identify. No, these screams echoed and popped, then drew themselves out longer and longer, as if the baby's mouth had opened up to scream at the sky. All the while, the rain went on and on, pounding and sputtering, the cracks of thunder almost providing a relief from the pitch of the baby's cries.

Earl and I lay side by side on the bed and breathed. We pulled the covers up to our chins and looked at the ceiling.

"Maybe I should go to him," I said finally, after what felt like an endless bout of silence between us.

"I don't think that would be wise. We don't know what he wants."

"Maybe he just wants some comfort. Or more food."

"Linda, he's eaten almost everything in the garden. There's no way he could be hungry."

"But look how hungry we were before, when we ate the way we did. Maybe parenthood makes you hungry."

"Is that what we are now? *Parents*?"

"I don't know," I said, because I didn't. "What would you call us, then?"

Earl pressed a hand over his eyes and rubbed his face again. I propped myself up on one elbow to get a better look at him. Even covered in dirt the way it was, Earl's face told me things I hadn't known before. It hadn't just been me this whole time. Earl, too, had gotten old. How had that happened? And why had it taken me so long to notice?

"I guess we're parents, then," he said.

"Then that makes me his mother," I said, and I pulled down the covers and sat up on the side of the bed, my back to Earl. "Babies need their mothers, Earl. Which is why I ought to go."

Earl threw back the covers all at once and stood up. He rushed into the bathroom before I could ask where he was going and came back washed and scrubbed, looking much more like the Earl I'd known all these years. Maybe he wasn't getting old after all, I thought. Maybe I wasn't either.

I shuffled past Earl and into the bathroom, where I splashed cold water on my face and scrubbed at the dirt on my cheeks and around my mouth with a washcloth. Just as I turned out the light in the bathroom, the baby let out a wail. I clutched my hands over my stomach to see if the burning had returned, but it was gone now. Absent. I rubbed my stomach harder to make the feeling return, that pull I'd felt when we'd first found the baby in the hole, but nothing came.

Still, we went out to him, Earl and I, with the rain bathing us in sheets, the whole yard soaked so that our feet made sucking sounds as we moved across the lawn to the garden gate. As I got closer, I could see the baby looking at me as I approached him, his eyes closed as he wailed in the rain.

"It's all right now," I said, moving closer to him. "There, there."

I took in the whole of him as the rain washed over me. Earl stood back as I reached out to the baby, who kept on screaming as I approached. The roots still jutted from his back in a tangle of vines the color of skin. Even through the rain I could see his face soften as I moved closer, the dirt soaking my legs as I kneeled down next to him and reached out to touch first his hand and then his face.

"There, there," I said again. "There, there."

I did my best to wrap my arms around him and held him there in the mud, careful not to disturb his roots. I turned toward Earl as I untangled the roots enough to let him lie against me, his head in my lap. Earl smiled at me and nodded. Just as he did, the rain stopped and, for a while, so did the screaming.

EIGHT

The next morning the baby stood as high as Earl.

Sometime during the night Earl had convinced me to leave him there in the garden. He'd been calm for hours with his bald head in my lap. His head was covered with a scattering of veins that pulsed when he breathed, and I'd spent hours watching the rise and fall of his chest, the pulsing of those veins. I hadn't slept at all, and there seemed little I could do for him sitting there in the garden with his giant head in my lap.

"He's resting now, and we should be, too," Earl said.

I did know that much. I'd heard that on a television show about newborns once. When the baby came, they'd told the mothers, the best thing to do was to sleep when the baby slept.

I didn't know how Earl knew this, but I was too exhausted to ask him. I'd managed to fall asleep for a short time on the Barcalounger with Earl on the floor next to me—I'd been afraid that I wouldn't hear the baby from the bedroom if he cried for me in the night—and when I woke up at dawn, the first thing I did was to go to the kitchen window for a look.

It was then that I saw him, bigger now, his head higher than the string beans we'd once tried to grow as corn. He sat with a pumpkin from the tree in his lap, his hands and face covered with orange as he scooped it up and shoved the chunks of pumpkin into his mouth.

Somehow I wasn't surprised by the sight of him, this baby now the size of a man, round-bellied with dimpled skin, sitting out there feeding himself one of our pumpkins. I don't know why I wasn't surprised, except that what could possibly surprise me after I'd spent half the night with a baby with roots in its back asleep in my lap?

I took some time to myself before I woke Earl. For a long while I stood at the window and watched the baby slobber happily on himself with fistfuls of pumpkin. During the night I'd waited for that peculiar burning in my stomach to return, but it hadn't come back, much as I'd wanted it to. Was this how it felt to be a mother? I wondered, looking out at the baby we'd grown from ten toes. Was it all a mixture of blur and sleeplessness, quick bursts of happiness and then more fatigue?

As the baby swung an arm to grab another of our pumpkins, I looked hard at his giant head and dimpled arms, the tight pouch of its belly. Did this baby really belong to us—to Earl and me— this baby still rooted to the earth? Could I really call myself its mother?

I sat down at the kitchen table and got out the seed catalog while Earl snored in the next room. I looked at the page filled with the roses that I'd found the day Earl came inside with the toes. I thought of the roses I'd imagined that we had grown, Earl and I, since we'd never had luck with anything in that garden of ours. But still we'd taken all of it—the pumpkins out of the tree and the eggplant shaped like baskets and the cucumbers thick as pythons—and now this baby grown the size of a man in three days' time.

I closed the seed catalog and was just about to go to wake Earl when I heard it.

"Maaaaaa!" the baby screamed. "Maaaaaa-maaaaa!"

I ran. I ran with Earl at my heels for the garden and saw the baby, covered in pumpkin seeds, his mouth open as he screamed. The baby that had lain his head in my lap just the night before looked different to me now, even in this soft morning light.

I can say it now. Now I can.

I was scared.

"There, there," I called, cupping my hands over my mouth and calling to him. "There, there now. There, there."

But the baby didn't look at me. He just kept sitting in the dirt with his head back, shrieking up at the sky.

I felt Earl reach for my hand. I thought of the day I'd heard Earl screaming when the backhoe turned on him, the blood spurting from his shorts and down his bare legs. I tried to think of what I'd said to Earl that day to comfort him, but all I remembered was the murmuring, my face against Earl's.

"Maaaa-maaaaa!"

The baby screamed some more.

"Say something, Linda," Earl said,

squeezing my hand again. "Say something to him."

I tried again.

"There, there," I said, shouting now. "There, there now!"

The baby did not look at me.

"There, there now!" I screamed so loud that the force of it burned my throat. "Here I am! Mama's here!"

I waved my arms over my head to try to get his attention, but the crying went on and on. I stood helpless as I watched the baby screaming, his face twisted up in anguish, tears spurting from his tightly closed eyes. I pressed my hands against my stomach and did the only thing I could think of to do. I moved forward and walked closer, closer, until I was close enough to reach him. Then I spread my arms wide and moved to wrap them around the giant torso, thickly smeared with pumpkin. I felt the baby's pulse racing against my neck and heard Earl coaching me from behind.

"That's it, Linda," he called. "Hold on to him now."

I closed my eyes and held. I brought my hands around the baby's back and felt at one of the roots. It was hard and sticky at once, spidery and warm.

"There, there," I said again.

And that's when the baby reared up and shoved me to the ground with his plump fists. He shoved me so hard my head hit the dirt with a thud. Pieces of pumpkin splattered me in the face.

He looked down at me as Earl came to pull me up by the shoulders, and in that instant, he opened his eyes, bluish eyes covered with a thin milky film. I saw nothing in those eyes and, I think it's fair to say, neither did the baby.

NINE

I was not, I told Earl, that baby's Mama.

"Then who is?" Earl asked. "Who is, then, if not you?"

We sat on the back lawn and watched as the baby devoured everything we'd grown. He started with the pumpkins, then worked his way through the raspberry bushes until finally he settled on the tomatoes as big as globes.

We spent the whole day watching the baby eat, which seemed to be the only thing that stopped him from screaming. We took turns going inside to the bathroom or making ourselves tea. Neither of us had eaten, and I can't speak for Earl, but I know that the last thing I felt was hungry.

"I don't know," I said, sighing. My whole body still ached from being shoved. "I just know it isn't me."

Earl didn't argue. I half-expected that he might try to convince me otherwise or tell me to try harder, forget the shove, be more nurturing. But he just nodded and rubbed his eyes. Then he pressed his hands over both of mine, the way he'd done with the toes, the same way he'd covered my hands with his own when we reached for the same carton of cherry tomatoes and he'd told me his name.

I cried then, looking down at our hands, and Earl began to cry, too. I leaned my head against his and let myself cry on the lawn while the giant baby ate and screamed, screamed and ate. I cried for Earl's being fired from the lumberyard and the wounds he still had from the backhoe, and I cried for the ache I felt every time I lay in bed with Earl and wished I could get inside him and hide myself there. I cried thinking of us together at the diner. Just us, the way it had always been. Just Earl and me.

I knew then what I had to do.

TEN

That night while Earl slept, I went about the business of growing a mother for the baby.

I had to wait until the baby was asleep as well, which wasn't easy because he would only doze off for a few minutes at a time before he started screaming again. For a long time I sat on the grass and just watched him, checking my watch to see how long he slept in between eating pumpkins and the squash that had ballooned out of the ground the one time we'd planted rhubarb. By my best account, he would spend fifteen minutes eating and then, when he was finished, he would pass out in the dirt for eighteen minutes precisely. That gave me eighteen minutes to do the job—eighteen minutes to plant.

I had my cutters and spade in the pockets of my apron, and once he was out, I snuck in next to him. I carried a small pencil flashlight, too, to avoid tripping over the pumpkin rinds. When I heard the puffs of breath coming out of his rounded mouth, I crawled through the dirt and got behind him to where the roots jutted out from his skin. As quietly as I could, I reached into the apron for the cutters and opened them around one of the fleshy roots. What if it hurt? I thought, as I held the cutters with one hand and the flashlight in the other. What if the baby bled? What would I do if I hurt this baby that Earl and I had grown?

I took in the deepest breath I could and pressed down on the cutters. The root felt hard, harder than I expected. I let go of the flashlight and took another deep breath, closed my eyes, and snapped the cutters closed. Once, twice, and on the second snap, I stifled the yelp on my lips where I'd cut myself.

The pain hit me, white and burning, but I knew I only had a few more minutes until the baby would start to feed again. I clipped a small piece of the root and cupped it in my palm. As I scrambled to dig a hole next to him, throwing up the dirt with my spade, I thought that this must be how mothers felt, always on edge. Or maybe, I thought, this was how I would have felt if I had ever become a mother the way other women did, always nervous and just a little bit in pain.

That wasn't the kind of mother I'd want to be, and that wasn't the kind of mother the baby deserved. I was a mother to all the things I'd grown, giant and strange as they were. I loved all the crazy things that the garden had sent us. Everything we'd grown belonged to Earl and me, but at the same time it didn't. Everything was ours and not ours all at once.

I dug a hole as deep as the one we'd dug for the baby. I dug by instinct, using my hands and the spade at the same time. When I thought the hole was large enough, I pressed the root of the baby into the earth. Then I threw dirt in handfuls into the hole and patted it down with both hands, the hand I'd cut throbbing all the time.

As soon as the hole was filled, the baby started to stir.

"There, there," I whispered, and then I ran from him, out of the garden and into the house, just as he started to scream.

While running water over my bloody hand in the kitchen sink, I saw that the tip of my index finger was gone.

I can't say that it hurt. Even as the water poured over the nub, the throbbing had stopped and with it came a numbness that started in the finger and traveled up through my palm. The blood filled the lines in my skin like webs. I stood there watching the blood follow the paths down into the space where the hand met my wrist. The blood pooled and stayed there, even when I lifted my hand to try to get the blood to drip down my arm. The one deep line in my palm seemed to gather up all the blood and push it down into the skin like roots.

And then it stopped. There at the sink with the stump of my ring finger still exposed, my hand stopped bleeding.

I knew then that the tip of my finger had fallen into the hole. Just like Earl that day with the backhoe, I had left a piece of myself in the garden. Earl had given his blood to the dirt, but mine, I knew, as I smiled to myself in the kitchen, had been given to the giant baby that Earl and I had grown.

As I shut off the water and padded back down the hallway to wake Earl, I stopped at the silence I hadn't heard since the baby first sprouted.

He'd stopped crying.

ELEVEN

The events of the next few days seemed to happen as if I were watching the world through gauze. We spent most of our time outside now that the giant baby had fallen into such a deep sleep. We got out our Adirondack chairs and watched him. Earl kept suggesting we wake the baby to eat, and when he wasn't worrying about the baby sleeping so much, he fretted about my hand. I kept trying to assure Earl that the hand was fine, that I rather liked the way my ring finger looked now. It had always been overly long, and now, with the tip of it cut away, it seemed to match the rest of my hand in a way it hadn't before. I didn't say anything else to Earl as I sat beside him.

"It's not just your hand and all this sleeping, Linda," he said, as the baby moved onto his back and snored against the cabbage. "Everything's so quiet. It's starting to get to me."

"There, there, Earl," I said, and patted his hand. "There, there."

I hadn't told him what I'd done that night. In all the years we'd been together, I hadn't ever kept anything from Earl. When he asked me how I'd cut my hand, I'd lied and said I'd been chopping some of the foot-long carrots for the baby. The idea of knowing something he didn't gave me a strange feeling that floated over me. When I looked at Earl, I blinked and blinked to try to make him come into focus, but he suddenly looked cloudy to me. Blurred.

"I think we should wake him up," he said again. "Feed him. Babies don't go this long without feeding, Linda. Even I know that much."

I touched the smooth end of the missing fingertip and smiled to myself. I thought about the famous episode of *I Love Lucy* where Lucy shows up to meet Ricky at the nightclub to tell him she's pregnant. She's gotten word to Ricky that someone in the audience is having a baby, and Ricky sings and sings, stopping at each table to ask, "Is it you?" I thought about Lucy sitting at the table alone, waiting for Ricky to ask her. I'd watched that episode hundreds of times, but only now did I know how Lucy felt, knowing something Ricky didn't, how satisfied and expectant she felt all at once.

I could have told Earl what I'd done, but just like Lucy, I didn't want to take away the surprise.

She rose up out of the earth the very next day.

The rumble shook the house, rattled the windows. We'd gone inside for more tea and a nap since we'd been watching the baby almost around the clock. I'd finally convinced Earl to go inside when he suggested that we bring the baby several gallon jugs of milk.

"How can you not be worried?" he said when I told him I didn't think a baby rooted to the ground ought to be drinking milk. "All he does is sleep now. Maybe the milk will help him grow."

"Do you really want to make him any bigger?" I asked. "Earl, be sensible. Milk can't be good for the soil."

"Well, we just have to risk the soil, then. No baby sleeps this long."

"He'll be fine, Earl. I'm telling you, he'll be fine. Let's go inside for a while and settle you down."

"How can you be so sure he'll be fine?"

"Instinct," I said. "Trust me."

So when she shot up from the ground, sending an explosion of dirt into the air, I felt something shift, something deep inside me that went all the way down to the bone. I held on to Earl's hand as she grew and grew before our eyes, and

I squeezed his hand with mine, the one with the missing fingertip. Neither of us said anything as she appeared, first her head and shoulders, then the thick swirl of dark hair, her arms and waist and knees. She was naked, and out of a show of respect, Earl shielded his eyes.

"Is she done?" he said when the eruption stopped. "Give her something to cover herself."

I let go of Earl's hand to move forward, but before I could, she reached down for a comforter that Earl and I had used to warm ourselves one night while we watched the baby sleep.

"Can I look now?" he asked. "Is it safe?"

I reached up and moved his hand away from his eyes.

Earl dropped to his knees in the dirt.

"My God, Linda," he said, his voice cracking, "she's a giant you."

TWELVE

I suppose she did look like me, but only vaguely. Many times since that day I've seen her face inside my mind and closed my eyes to hold it there, but the image always slips away. Earl still swears that the garden produced a giant version of me, though I've never told him about what I did, cutting the baby's roots and leaving a piece of my finger in the dirt that night. Her eyes were brown where mine are green, and she had fierce dimples that showed in the one moment when she smiled at me.

Earl doesn't remember what happened after she rose up out of the ground, though I've tried my best to tell him. I've told him how she reached down with her long white arms and lifted the sleeping baby up, how the roots made a soft splitting sound I can still hear at night when I lie against Earl and press my face into his back. I tell him how she held the baby against her in a way we never could, and how the baby turned his face up to hers. I tell him that she stepped in pieces of pumpkin as she lifted first one foot and then the other out of the ground, and how I wish I'd had the good sense to go inside for a camera to save the image of the orange footprints she left behind in the grass.

"But you were out cold, and my mind was on you, Earl," I say, "the way it always is."

When I say that last part he kisses me,

and we press ourselves together and hold on, the way we have since the beginning.

For a while we missed the giant baby, and it seemed that he was all we had to talk about anymore—how we'd planted the toes like a blessing, how we'd found him that day, so tiny in the dirt. How we tried to pull him out. How we watched him eat and scream and sleep, all of the hours we spent waiting and watching and feeding. How big he'd grown over-night, and how he was ours and not ours, like everything in the garden. How she rose up out of the soil and took him away, and how sometimes we still miss him.

Then, just as suddenly as the baby had grown and changed everything, one day we started talking about other things,

things we used to talk about. Seeds. Soil. The strangeness of our garden.

"Let's try roses," Earl said one Sunday in the car on our way to the town diner. "Maybe we'll have better luck with flowers."

I just smiled to myself and thought of the day Earl had come to me with the toes, how he'd opened his hands and showed them to me , how we'd been so full of hope.

I looked down at the space where a piece of my finger was missing and felt the nub throb the way it did whenever we talked about the giant baby. As we got out of the car and waited to be seated, I looked at the families and smiled. A baby in a high chair banged his spoon on the table. I raised my hand, the one still intact, and waved at him.

"Well, well," the waitress said when she seated us in our old spot in the back, near the kitchen. "I was beginning to wonder about the two of you."

We just laughed. Earl reached across the table and ran his fingers over the missing the tip, as we waited for the waitress to bring us our coffee and cheese danishes. From where I was sitting I could still see the baby in the next room. He smiled at me, showing his gums. I smiled back and then turned to Earl, who gave me his best Earl smile, the lopsided one, the one he saved only for me.

We sat there waiting. Earl and me. Me and Earl. Just us.